Little
Skink's
Tail

By Janet Halfmann   Illustrated by Laurie Allen Klein

With love to my granddaughter Monae, a bundle of inspiration—JH
To Bob & Jesse—LAK

Thanks to Sherry Crawley, Director of Education, School and Family Programs
at Zoo Atlanta for verifying the accuracy of the information in this book.

Publisher's Cataloging-In-Publication Data

Halfmann, Janet.
Little Skink's tail / by Janet Halfmann ; illustrated by Laurie Allen Klein.

p. : col. ill. ; cm.

Summary: While Little Skink hunts for breakfast, she is attacked by a crow and escapes by
snapping off her tail. Little Skink's Tail follows her as she daydreams of having the tails of other
animals in the forest. Includes "For Creative Minds" section with information on tail adaptations,
matching activity, and a footprint map activity.
Interest age level: 004-008.
Interest grade level: P-3.
ISBN: 978-0-9768823-8-1 (hardcover)
ISBN: 978-1-934359-20-4 (pbk.)

1. Skinks--Juvenile fiction. 2. Tail--Juvenile fiction. 3. Skinks--Fiction. 4. Tail--Fiction.
I. Klein, Laurie Allen. II. Title.

PZ10.3.H136 Li 2007[E]   2007920038

Printed in China

Sylvan Dell Publishing
976 Houston Northcutt Blvd., Suite 3
Mt. Pleasant, SC 29464

Little Skink basked on a big yellow rock in
the rays of the morning sun.
Her chilly body soon turned snugly warm.
She twitched her bright blue tail.

The little lizard was ready to start her day.

Leaping to the forest floor,
she poked her pointy
nose into a crack in a rotting log
and looked for breakfast.
Sniff, sniff! She smelled ants.

She loved ants!

Gobble, gobble, gobble.
**She gulped down
one ant after another.**

Her tummy was almost full
when she felt a peck on her tail.
It was a large, hungry crow!

Little Skink was trapped. There was no way to run. But she had a trick . . .

Quicker than the crow could blink,
Little Skink snapped off her bright blue tail!

Wiggle, waggle, wiggle,
went the tail,
wriggling wildly through
the fallen leaves.

The crow forgot all about Little Skink.
It wanted that wiggling, waggling tail!

As the crow bounced
this way and that,
Little Skink slinked under a log.
She was safe.

Her wiggling, waggling tail had saved her.

The next morning, as
Little Skink basked on her rock,
she felt a little sad.

She missed her bright blue tail, even
though she was happy to be alive.

As she lay
basking and thinking,
a cottontail rabbit
hopped in front of her rock.

"Hmmm, I wonder how I'd look with
a tail like that?" Little Skink thought.

**She pictured her new look.
"Very cute," she thought to herself,
"but too *puffy-fluffy*."**

Next, she tried a squirrel's tail:
"It's fun to flick and fluff," she said,
"but much too bushy."

Day after day,
Little Skink imagined herself
wearing the tail
of every animal she met.

A deer's tail: "Look! I can wave it like a little flag," she said. "But it's so short and stubby."

A skunk's tail:
"Peeeuuw!" said Little Skink.
"Stinky stinky stinky!"

A porcupine's tail:
"Too *stickly-prickly*," she said.

An owl's tail:
"A lizard with feathers?"
she exclaimed.

"I don't think so!"

A turtle's tail:
"Too pointy," said Little Skink.

While all were fine tails,
not one was quite right for her.

Then one day as she
scampered onto her sunny rock,
her shadow caught her eye . . .

Her shadow had a tail!

She whipped around.
Sure enough,
her tail had grown back.

"A skink needs a skink's tail," she said,
and her tail-dreaming days were over.

For Creative Minds

Footprint Map

Using the animal footprints as hints, can you identify where Little Skink saw the animals in the woods? Find the number and the letter of the box that identifies the animal tracks. For example, Little Skink is located in box 7, D.

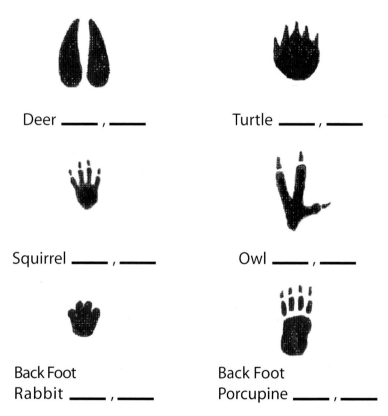

Deer ____ , ____

Turtle ____ , ____

Squirrel ____ , ____

Owl ____ , ____

Back Foot
Rabbit ____ , ____

Back Foot
Porcupine ____ , ____

1. If Little Skink starts at her rock (7, D), how many squares would she have to walk to find turtle and in which direction?

2. How many squares would turtle go to find porcupine and in which direction?

3. Which animal is to the northwest of Little Skink?

Answers:
Deer:1,J; Turtle:7,G; Squirrel:5,A; Owl:3,K; Rabbit:4,E; Porcupine:2,G; 1. 3 squares to the east; 2. 5 squares to the north; 3. the squirrel